D0547252

Dear Emmy
I really hope you enjoy the book.
Love,
Harpreet Dayal

Wilbert the Worm

Harpreet M Dayal

Illustrated by Joanna Scott

Text copyright © Harpreet M Dayal, 2016

Illustrations copyright © Joanna Scott, 2016

Sanvaad Publishing House

Harpreet M Dayal and Joanna Scott assert the moral right to be identified as the author and illustrator of this work. All rights reserved.

No part of this book may be reproduced, distributed or transmitted in any form or by any means, including photocopying, recording, or other electronic methods, without the written permission of the author.

ISBN 978-0-9950527-0-3

This book is dedicated to

My parents, who have shaped me
the many shapes I am today.

My siblings, with whom I have lived
my childhood stories. I love you.

My husband, my love, my all, who has
taught me self-love and self-belief.

Lastly, I dedicate this book to my late grandfather,
who had his fair share of adventures and
has inspired me to have mine as well.

Chapter 1

Wilbert the Worm

IN A BEAUTIFUL GARDEN, there was a flower bed. It was covered with red roses and yellow daisies. Among these flowers, there was a small hole in the dirt and mud. Past this small hole, deep below the ground, lived a worm. His name was Wilbert. You could find his home in a tiny tunnel beside a big round stone.

Wilbert was a quiet and shy worm. He had big round eyes and a warm smile. His cheeks were always glowing pink. He enjoyed being underground so much that he would take the same familiar route through the dirt. He would wake up every morning and travel only a little further from home to a place made of a pile of stones that were of all shapes and colors.

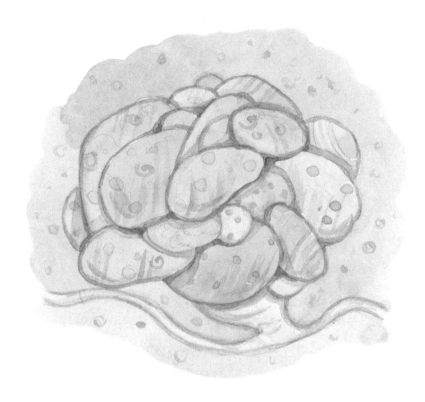

He called it the stone mound. He would crawl through the dirt to the stone mound to admire it and then make his way back home. Apart from home, this was one of his favourite places. Wilbert's friend Amy playfully named it Wilby's Route because it is the only way Wilbert ever travelled. Some days he would crawl slowly, enjoying the feel of the earth. Other days, when he

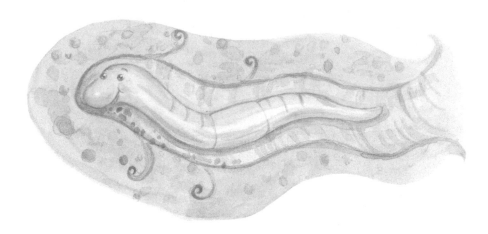

felt very daring, he would rush as if swimming through water. Although Wilbert enjoyed being underground, he also had a secret desire. He had always wanted to go above ground to see what it was like. There were many times he thought of trying, but he never did. He had become so comfortable and used to living deep in the ground.

Then, on a day like any other, Wilbert the

Worm set off to make his usual trip along his dirt track singing to himself.

Off I go

Crawling through the dirt I go

Off I go

Digging through the dirt I go

One pebble, two pebbles, three

Oh yes! These are all for me!

Off I go

Crawling through the dirt I go

Off I go

Digging through the dirt I go

Four pebbles, five pebbles, six

Oh what a beautiful,

colorful mix

Off I go

Crawling through the dirt I go…

Chapter 2

Amy the Ant

HIS SONG WAS CUT short by the familiar scurrying of his dear friend, Amy the Ant. Wilbert didn't have a lot of friends, the only real friend he had was Amy. Amy was a very small brown ant with beautiful antennae. Wilbert's friend had the friendliest big black eyes and a wide smile to match.

As the scurrying of her long legs grew closer, Wilbert thought of how much he admired his dear friend. She was quite different from how he was. Where he was quiet and comfortable, she was loud and confident. She was worldly. She had travelled far and wide underground, more than Wilbert ever had. She'd travelled deeper underground, but she had also travelled past the roots of trees and flowers

that grew above the surface. 'Ah, Wilbert!' yelled Amy as she came scurrying towards him.

'Hello Amy!' Wilbert smiled. 'What brings you down this way today?'

Amy grinned at Wilbert and began scurrying back towards the path Wilbert had come from. 'I have a lot to tell you, Wilbert! I went up to the surface yesterday

and wow, the things I saw!' Wilbert
followed Amy as she continued talking.
Although he still smiled, he couldn't help
feel a little sad. He had nothing exciting to
tell her. Amy stopped in front of Wilbert's
home. He crawled through the tiny tunnel
next to the stone and Amy followed. As
soon as they were inside, Amy began
dancing around. Wilbert took a seat in his
chair, looking slightly startled. His chair
was made from a pile of dirt that he had
collected and squished together. He made
his bed the same way too. 'What were you
going to tell me?' he asked. Amy finally sat
on the floor in front of him. She paused for
a moment as if gathering her thoughts and
memories. All of a sudden she broke into a
song, singing of her adventures!

I was scurrying

Through the rich green grass

There were flowers scattered like paint

Red roses and yellow daisies

The sun was shining, sparkling bright

Then I felt a drop

A drop of rain

It fell between my eyes

I couldn't help but smile wide!

Rain began falling

Drops began forming

On strands of grass

They looked like pearls made of glass

I heard all of a sudden

The flutter of great big wings

Deep purple and bright blue wings!

It was one of my good friends

Betty the Butterfly!

'Amy!' she said, 'look above the roses

and daisies, you'll see an arch!'

Oh, Wilbert, you would not believe it!

Etched across the light sky

An arch made of lovely colours

Red, orange, yellow and green!

But that's not all

There was blue, indigo and violet too!

Glistening in the shining sun

and splattering rain

The most amazing

and mystifying thing I'd seen!

The most beautiful rainbow!

'Well that's quite the adventure, Amy,' Wilbert said. He was astonished by Amy's enthusiasm and energy. 'Yes! There is plenty more, Wilbert, but it will have to be for another time. I have a lot to do before tomorrow!' She grinned and twirled around with excitement.

Amy made her way out of the tunnel. Wilbert smiled at the wide-eyed Amy and

bid her goodbye, until next time. When she was gone Wilbert went straight to bed. He lay down but found that he could not sleep. He found himself daydreaming about the things that were on the surface. How he would like to see the blue sky and different colored flowers. He'd often wondered what they would smell like. He would love to see a butterfly and even talk to one. He smiled as he imagined the colors of the rainbow that Amy had told him about. Eyes closed, he could hear Amy's song. Wilbert pictured the rain drizzling lightly and the sun shining brightly. He tried to imagine the beautiful arch made of all the different colors. But along with these daydreams there was a voice inside him that told him no. Why would he want to go all the way

up there? He had never been up to the surface before. What if he got lost? What if he couldn't find his way up? What if he saw things he had never seen before? With all these thoughts swirling in his mind he eventually drifted off to sleep.

Chapter 3

Shaun the Spider, Darren the Digger Bee and The Ditch

THE NEXT DAY, WILBERT got out of bed as he did every morning. He felt tired because he had not slept very well. He had been thinking of all the stories Amy had told him. Again, Wilbert set off on his usual route, humming his usual song. But then he saw a tiny tunnel to his right. He had not seen it before.

Where he would normally carry on crawling forward, he couldn't help but wonder what it would be like to start digging a new path and where it may lead. He closed his eyes and gulped, and he felt a weird sensation in the pit of his stomach. He quivered a little and felt scared as he jumped into the tunnel on his right and began to dig. Wilbert found that the dirt

tasted different, better! But he felt the familiarity of the old path tugging at him and he felt the strongest urge to turn back. So Wilbert turned his head back, but his body hadn't fully caught up with his head. He tripped on something and fell with a thud into a small ditch. He coughed and spluttered, choking on the dirt. His head swam, so he focused on a little light ahead of him until everything around him stopped moving.

As Wilbert's surroundings came into focus, he jumped as he heard the sound of snickering coming from behind him. Dangling from a spider web, on top of a mound made of dirt was a large, bulky spider. The spider had a big round body with eight quivering thin black pincers. He had a tiny head and small beady eyes that looked left and right quickly out of habit. It made him look permanently nervous.

He continued to snicker away. Next to him hovering mid-air was a rather big bee. 'You all right there, little man?' the spider said in a deep voice. He seemed to be guarding something. The spider scuttled down from the mound. Wilbert squinted as he tried to make out what the bee looked like, but he was finding it difficult to do so. There was a light streaming from behind the bee. As Wilbert continued to squint into the bright light, the bee flew closer to Wilbert. He was

a rather round, hairy bee. He had a protruding mean-looking face. While his furry body had a tinge of blue, his face was a dark yellow. He was no ordinary bee. He was a digger bee. The Digger Bee didn't fly above ground but lived alone under the surface.

As Wilbert sat still on the ground, the digger bee began buzzing around him. Round and round he would buzz while the silly spider continued to snicker. Wilbert was getting very dizzy. He shook his head and began to wriggle to where he had fallen from. As he got closer, the big bee stopped buzzing. He soared and flapped his tiny wings in front of Wilbert and said, 'why are you in such a rush to leave, Wormy?'

The spider was smirking in the background.
He came scuttling up by his friend's side.

Wilbert stared at them both a little while.
Realizing he was staring for a lot longer
than he had intended, Wilbert quickly
looked away. Instead, he gaped up at the
hole he had fallen out from.

As he continued to stare upwards, he said,

'my name is Wilbert, not Wormy.' All he had to do was crawl up a little and make his way back. He'd be home in no time, he thought to himself. 'Well since you didn't ask, I'll just introduce myself, shall I? My name is Darren and this is my friend Shaun.' Darren the Digger Bee buzzed past Wilbert and began buzzing around his friend Shaun. 'You can stop laughing now!' yelled Darren abruptly. Shaun twitched a

little and stood still. He looked at Darren buzzing around and whispered, 'sorry.' Darren laughed and bee-lined towards Wilbert again. 'You aren't from around here, are you Wilbert?' he grinned. 'I mean, I certainly haven't seen you around here.'

Wilbert did not like Darren. He was rude and harsh. You can tell a lot about someone by the way they treat others, especially their friends. Wilbert moved his gaze away from the annoying bee and looked at Shaun. The spider looked disheartened. Both Wilbert and Shaun exchanged a glance but they quickly turned away. Shaun began scuttling around, eyeing the ground closely, looking for food.

'Hello?!' yelled Darren the Digger Bee. Wilbert jumped a little and Shaun froze. Wilbert was getting nervous. He turned towards Darren and he began rambling with great speed. 'Yes I am not from around here and I don't really know how I ended up here.'

'I know you're not from around here,' said Darren with a menacing grin, 'so you were obviously not heading home. Where were you going?'

'I was going above…' Wilbert trailed off mid-sentence as he felt his cheeks burning. He had the feeling that it wasn't a good idea if Darren and his friend Shaun knew where he was travelling to. 'You were going above ground?' Darren smiled. He was buzzing

inches closer to Wilbert now. 'Have you been above ground before?' asked Darren. Wilbert could sense that Darren already knew what the answer was. He could feel his face turn red as Darren's face grew smug. Shaun stopped looking for food and scuttled closer to Darren. 'Hey Darren, it seems like Wormy *was* going above ground! I mean look at his face. I've never seen a worm's face so red. He looks like a tomato!' Darren grinned at Wilbert and burst into a song.

Buzz, buzz!

Scuttle, scuttle!

I can't help but chuckle!

Wormy, Wormy!

Why so squirmy?

Were you up bright and early?

Buzz, buzz!

Scuttle, scuttle!

You even dug that tunnel?

Oh, I can't help but chuckle!

Wormy, Wormy!

Why so squirmy?

Did you really plan this journey?

Buzz, buzz!

Scuttle, scuttle!

I've heard you live in your bubble

I can't help but chuckle!

Wormy! Wormy!

Why so squirmy?

Do you think that you are worldly?

But Wormy, Wormy

Or Wilbert

is it?

Why is your face so red?

Is it a fear unsaid?

Shaun scuttled around repeating the song while Darren buzzed around chuckling. Wilbert's face began to tingle from the heat. Why did he decide to turn into the new tunnel? Now he had to deal with these two bullies. The buzzing bee was rolling on the ground laughing, his tiny wings quivering.

While the two bullies were busy laughing, Wilbert looked up again from where he had fallen. Face still tingling, he crawled as fast he could over the sloping dirt into the hole he had made. Feeling disappointed in himself, he crawled his way home the same way he always did.

That night he slept a restless sleep. He dreamt of Darren and Shaun laughing and taunting him. In the dream, Wilbert felt very small while Darren and Shaun looked so big. They were telling him what was up there. All the things he hadn't seen. Then, Amy showed up out of nowhere. Standing next to him, she whispered into his ear, 'look towards that light, can you see it behind them? You have to get past them.'

With those words she vanished into thin air. Wilbert was shocked by her sudden disappearance and almost jumped out of his skin when Darren and Shaun drew closer and closer, laughing and cackling at him. The laughing grew louder and louder. Louder and louder still, until Wilbert woke

from his dream frightened and out of breath. He had never had such a bad dream before.

Chapter 4

Amy's Story

THE NEXT DAY WILBERT got up and he decided to go spend the day at the stone mound. So he went with secret dreams in his heart and images of beautiful things that existed above ground. And that's all they will be, he thought to himself. He didn't believe that he could ever reach the top.

As Wilbert came closer to the mound he heard the marching of ants. His heart sank a little. He really didn't want the company, but he heard the familiar voice of his dear friend Amy. 'Wilbert! It's so good to see you!' she yelled. The noise from the marching ants began to lessen as Amy scuttled back towards Wilbert's home. Amy noticed Wilbert's sullen face. She frowned and asked, 'what's wrong with you?'

When they reached Wilbert's home, Amy wasn't dancing as she usually did. Wilbert seemed down and the light in his happy face was out. He caught her staring at him with a pitiful look. 'Why are you looking at me like that?' he mumbled.

'Oh nothing, Wilbert, you haven't asked me about my adventure. I have a lot to tell you,' Amy said, waiting for him to reply.

Wilbert crawled over to sit in his chair as he said, 'I'm sorry, Amy. I forgot to ask. Do go ahead and tell me.' He wasn't as enthusiastic as he normally was and Amy could see this. She sighed and said, 'something has happened and you're not telling me. I am your friend Wilbert, you can tell me. Maybe I can help you?'

The worm looked at Amy's wide-eyed face for a little while and after taking a deep breath he murmured, 'I decided to take a little detour yesterday. I took a different route than my usual... I was trying to go

above ground.' Wilbert looked at Amy gingerly, blushing. Amy couldn't believe Wilbert's words. 'Really?' said Amy, 'but you love living deep in the dirt!'

'Yes, I know! I just wanted to do something new,' grumbled Wilbert. 'It doesn't matter now anyway,' he continued, 'you were telling me about your recent adventure. Please tell me.'

Amy scuttled over to sit in front of Wilbert. He couldn't help but smile at her face. 'I'll tell you a story, Wilbert. I never tell you stories, I only tell you where I've been and what I've seen, but today I am going to tell you a story about someone.' Wilbert nodded for her to continue. She cleared her throat and began her story. 'Someone is a very good and kind person. He is quiet and he likes his routine.' Wilbert frowned a little but let her carry on. 'But one day *someone* decided that he wanted to see new and different things. *Someone* wanted to go above ground.'

Amy paused and observed Wilbert's face. He wouldn't make eye contact, but he fidgeted in his chair. Amy cleared her throat again and said, 'so someone decided to take a trip that he has never taken before. To go somewhere, he has never been before! But someone wasn't sure he could do it... he was even a little scared.'

'He wasn't scared!' cried Wilbert. Amy giggled as Wilbert continued, 'it's just others got in the way! They laughed at him and poked fun at him.'

'Okay? So someone wasn't scared. He was upset?' Amy didn't let Wilbert answer the question but said, 'Wilbert, you must let me finish my story.' He chuckled as he felt a little lighter. He let his friend carry on with her story although he knew she was talking about him. 'So *someone* was upset that others laughed at him and because of this he was sad for days and he rarely smiled. Someone decided that he will give up and never try again.' Amy looked at Wilbert's face as he sat in his chair. He was deep in thought with his eyes on the floor. There was silence for a little while until Amy cleared her throat for the third time. 'Will someone give up? Or will someone try again?' Wilbert looked up at her and Amy looked directly into his eyes.

'You're right, Amy... since when did you become so wise?' Amy got up and began scuttling around Wilbert's house excitedly. She promised that she would be back to visit soon and, this time, she would listen to

Wilbert's adventures.

Chapter 5

Past the Stone Mound

THE NEXT MORNING WILBERT decided to go past the stone mound to see what he would find. There was a tiny gap that he used to look through sometimes when he visited. He had noticed beyond the stone mound there were roots and weeds. They always looked so tempting to eat, but he never dared to dig further.

He was too afraid he would get lost if he went in an unknown direction. But now he smiled broadly at the food that was waiting for him. So he began to dig past the stone mound. He found the dirt, being untouched, was harder to swim through. He dug diagonally, making it easier and more likely for him to get above ground.

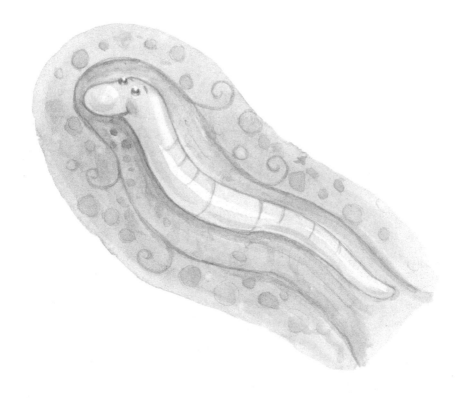

The dirt tasted delicious and nothing like he had tasted before. It had all these flavors and textures that were new to him. Higher and higher he went, swallowing the dirt he had loosened. It was as if he was climbing a mountain, digging at a steady speed. He imagined moving closer and closer above ground. He could imagine what the grass would smell like and what it would feel like for the sun to shine on his skin.

His daydream came to a standstill as he crashed into something hard. Wilbert shook his head, waiting for the stars to disappear before his eyes. Breathing heavily, he looked up and down at what he had crashed into. Whatever it was, it was covered in dirt. Looking closer, Wilbert

could see light brown and white roots sprouting in all directions like spider webs. He tried to dig into whatever was blocking his way. The dirt didn't crumble and beads of sweat trickled down his face. He tried again and again. And again! With every try, his heart sank. He collapsed against whatever was blocking his way. Tired and irritated, he closed his eyes and leaned his face against it. He had worked so hard all day climbing higher and higher only to be faced with this big wall. He opened his eyes and turned his head to look closely at the wall. Upon closer inspection, he realised that what he had crashed into was, in fact, an enormous root of a tree! Amy had told him about these so many times. She found them at the most random places when she was off marching. But lucky for her, she was small and she could climb up the tree to reach above ground.

Wilbert would have to turn back and find another way. Who knows how big this tree root was and Wilbert didn't have the energy to find out.

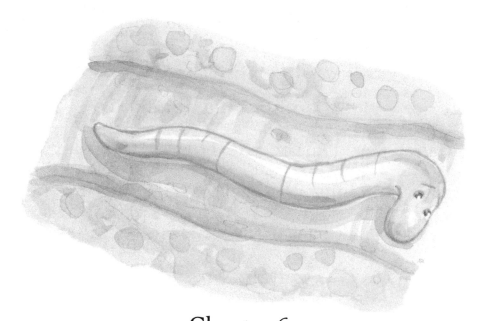

Chapter 6

The Pestering Bullies

WILBERT CRAWLED BACK DOWN this mountain he had climbed, feeling disheartened. It was getting late and he had decided that for now he was done for the day. As he slowly made his way back home, he thought he heard a soft buzzing from behind. He stopped and turned quickly, but he couldn't see anything behind him.

Shrugging his shoulders, he turned to go home but he heard the same buzzing sound. It drew closer and became louder! He knew that it was Darren the Digger Bee playing tricks on him. Wilbert carried on moving forward while looking behind him as he went. He was getting very annoyed by the buzzing sound. Darren was close by but he just couldn't see him.

All of a sudden Darren flew towards Wilbert at full speed. Wilbert was startled to find Darren's face inches from his when he turned to look ahead. 'Hello Wormy!' bellowed Darren. Taken by surprise, Wilbert fell to the ground. He could hear the scuttling of Shaun's pincers in the distance drawing closer to him. Darren began flying round and round Wilbert again. But Wilbert ignored the buzzing as he carried on crawling home. The familiar snickering of Shaun had also begun. Wilbert shot Shaun an angry look and Shaun stopped snickering.

As soon as Wilbert looked away, the snickering started up again. 'Wormy? Why

so mad?' Darren exchanged an amused look with Shaun. 'You look like you've had a long day.' Wilbert didn't say anything. Shaun said to Darren, 'I think he's been trying to go above ground!' Darren stopped buzzing around Wilbert's head and cackled mid-air. 'Why Wormy, is this true?' He smirked and buzzed around to face Wilbert, glaring at him. 'So did you really try to go above ground... again?'

Wilbert tried his best to ignore him. He wriggled his way around Darren, continuing to make his trip back. 'You don't have it in you to do it! So are you going to tell us or not? Is what Shaun saying true?' yelled Darren from behind.

Wilbert couldn't control himself much longer. He turned to face the both of them and said very loudly, 'yes! It's true!' Shaun stopped snickering, surprised by Wilbert. Even Darren stopped cackling for a moment. He flew closer to Wilbert until their faces were only inches apart, and he whispered, 'really?' Wilbert did not say a single word. He did not respond to Darren's question, but he looked straight ahead, past

Darren and Shaun and began crawling in the opposite direction. He was no longer going home. The bullies exchanged a confused look and followed Wilbert with their curious eyes. Wilbert knew what he wanted to do and where he was going.

He could hear the buzzing bee and the scuttling spider following him. They didn't say anything to him but he could hear their soft whispering. Their muttering was like the nagging inside Wilbert's head, questioning whether he could even do this. He had finally crawled back to where he had fallen into the ditch a few days ago.

With their eyes on him, he began to dig his way back to the ditch. He took his time so that he didn't fall again. He could hear the hushed sounds coming from behind him and he gulped as he felt heat rising in his face. A part of him was regretting being so brave. Maybe he should have just gone home.

The whispering from behind grew louder and louder but he knew he had to ignore it. He continued to dig with uncertainty fluttering around in his head and then he saw the ditch down below. He heard a distant huff from the digger bee. Darren the Digger Bee wasn't pleased. Wilbert took a deep breath and made the hole bigger so he could peer into it, the ditch didn't seem far down. The last time he was here, he hadn't been expecting to fall in. There was no more room for thinking now. He poked his head through the dirt. With another deep breath, and without looking back at the bullies, he leaped into the ditch, landing perfectly. Wilbert dusted himself off and looked around him, pondering what to do next.

Chapter 7

Back to the Ditch

WILBERT REALLY HADN'T HAD time to take in his surroundings last time. He hadn't thought of going above ground from here. As he gathered his thoughts, he heard the bullies behind him now. Shaun and Darren had made their way down through the hole too.

They were mumbling to each other very loudly as they crept closer. The last time Wilbert was here, Darren was hovering high above a mound and there was a bright light creeping in from behind him. Wilbert knew where he had to go and soon he would be where he had always dreamt of going. The ditch was silent now. There was no more muttering. Wilbert's gaze settled on

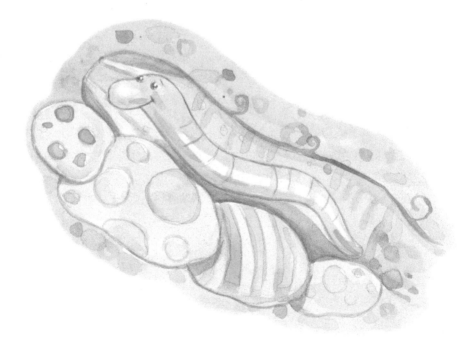

the very large mound across the ditch. It was very hard to miss. He was surprised it hadn't been the first thing he saw. As he began to slowly edge his way closer to the mound, he abruptly stopped in his tracks. There was a very loud gasp from behind him. The muttering continued. It was very hurried and angry. Wilbert wondered why they had not stopped him yet. Or even yelled names at him? Or told him he was silly for going up there?

Wilbert closed his eyes and took a deep breath as he continued to crawl up towards the mound until he finally reached the top. Wilbert looked at the dirt. It was covered in green weeds. He had rarely ever seen any green deep in the ground before. He looked up a little higher to where the light should have been coming from. He was just about to wriggle up towards it but was stopped by Darren, who came flying from behind. 'You don't even know what's up there!' exclaimed Darren with an air of panic in his voice. He seemed annoyed. Wilbert grinned at Darren. 'You're right; I don't know what's up there. But I have a fair idea and I am

willing to find out,' Wilbert told him. Panic vanished from Darren's face and quickly turned into an unkind sneer. Darren began buzzing around Wilbert like he always did. Shaun scuttled up from the background. Wilbert ignored them and focused his attention on where the source of light was coming from last time. He started crawling again with speed and determination. He crawled closer and closer to where the source of light had come from. His breathing became heavier. He had come so far and he was so close. He wasn't going to give up now. But Wilbert was caught and tangled in long strands of green weed.

As Wilbert untangled himself from the weeds he saw Darren soaring speedily towards him! Surprised, Wilbert ducked, and instead of flying into him, Darren ploughed into Shaun, who had scuttled up behind. Shaun shrieked loudly and was now lying flat on his back. He was moving his pincers, frantically trying to get back up.

'Get up you stupid spider!' yelled Darren. 'You don't want him to get up there, do you?' Darren shot a defeated look up at Wilbert. He began nudging Shaun in an effort to try and help him get back up but he wasn't doing a very good job. 'I'm trying Darren!' Shaun squealed. Wilbert ignored the squeals from down below and turned back around. Wilbert grinned as he stood in front of tiny specks of light shining through a hole.

Chapter 8

Above the Surface

WITH A BIG GULP of warm air, Wilbert popped his head up into the tiny hole. He squinted, blinded by the bright sun shining on him. He had never smelt air so fresh before. Wilbert had yet to see all the things he had waiting for him. All the things he had longed to see. He struggled a little as he crawled further and further towards the bright sunlight.

Huffing and puffing, he could not believe he was lying on the ground facing down, his eyes closed. He lifted his head a little and squinted at the softness on which he lay. It was fresh green, sprinkled with droplets of water that sparkled in the sun like diamonds. He moved his face closer to the green grass and breathed in deeply. He took another deep breath and remembered Amy's song and how she had described the grass and rain. It was exactly how he had imagined, but more.

His thoughts were interrupted by the sound of something flying above him. Wilbert turned around so he was now lying on the grass facing up at the blue sky. Amongst the sky and white clouds, floating in mid-air

63

was the most beautiful creature he had ever
seen. The most striking deep purple and
bright blue wings were fluttering in the sky
and a kind face was looking down at him.
Still in awe, mouth wide open, Wilbert
uttered, 'Betty?' Betty looked at Wilbert
more carefully and a moment later a smile
spread across her face. She fluttered closer
to Wilbert and landed gently on to a yellow

daisy. Astonished by the flower, he took in his surroundings more carefully. He had been so absorbed in admiring the grass that he didn't even look up at what was around him. He was surrounded by a field of red roses and yellow daisies which seemed to stretch on forever, just like Amy had said.

'It's gorgeous isn't it, Wilbert?' Wilbert took a moment to snap out of it and look up at Betty. 'You know who I am?' Wilbert asked.

'Of course, I know who you are,' sang Betty as she fluttered to another flower. Sitting on her perch, she gazed at Wilbert and said, 'your face gave it away!'

Puzzled, Wilbert questioned, 'what do you mean, Betty?'

'Well,' said Betty, still smiling, 'I've not seen anyone admire the grass, stare at the sky and the flowers quite like you. You haven't travelled above ground before, have you?' Wilbert felt his cheeks burning. He looked down at the glittering raindrops as he said, 'yes this is the first time I've seen the green grass and colorful flowers.'

Betty smiled with enthusiasm. 'You can join

me and we can explore the fields. You have a lot to see.'

'You would do that?' Wilbert smiled, feeling thankful. Betty was no longer perched on a flower but fluttering in the clear sky, ready to go. 'Of course and our friend Amy will be here at any moment too. She will be pleased to see you finally made it.'

Wilbert crawled behind Betty. He dug and sped through the surface of the grass and dirt. He was trying to keep up with Betty who fluttered ahead. Wilbert still couldn't believe he had made it this far.

He was singing Amy's song in his head as he saw all the things she had described. They had only travelled a little further when Wilbert heard the familiar sound of hurried scuttling. Wilbert looked ahead into the flowers. Betty could be heard fluttering above, laughing. 'I don't think we have to wait too long to see Amy!' Betty laughed. She perched herself next to Wilbert on one of the flowers once again. Looking at Wilbert, she said, 'it's better that we wait

here, and she'll find us soon enough... Amy, is that you I hear?

Amy appeared, rushing through the jungle of grass and flowers. She didn't say hello but looking delighted she scuttled around and around Betty and Wilbert. 'You made it, Wilbert! See Betty, I told you! I knew he would.' Wilbert grinned at his friend and Betty smiled back, adding, 'I didn't doubt it either.' Amy danced around Wilbert, excited. 'There is so much to see and so much to do! I'm so pleased you didn't listen to the bullies and came anyway... we will show you around. Won't we, Betty? And we will go to Betty's house and then...'

'Calm down, Amy!' interrupted Betty. 'Are you even breathing? There is plenty of time; Wilbert has only just got here. Let him take in his surroundings.' Amy scuttled ahead at a slow pace while Betty fluttered along beside her. Wilbert crawled and dug through the surface behind them, in awe of this new world around him. He didn't know where he was going but he followed his friends. Then he felt a drop of rain hit his head. One drop became two, two drops became three. The rain began to drizzle. The long blades of grass and the many flowers were shining

and sparkling with raindrops. Wilbert looked up at the sky and tried to look directly at the bright sun. He hadn't realised he had stopped. He had lived beneath the surface too long and knew that it was worth the entire struggle to get here.

He was too busy admiring the beauty around him to notice that Betty and Amy were on either side of him now. Betty was fluttering her great big wings mid-air; Amy was sitting surprisingly still. At that moment she whispered in Wilbert's ear, 'look ahead there Wilbert.' Wilbert dragged his eyes away from the sky and looked straight ahead, across the field. There behind the millions of red and yellow flowers, beyond the blades of green, etched on the perfect blue sky was the most stunning rainbow Wilbert had ever seen. Wilbert sighed and Amy asked, 'what's the matter, Wilbert?'

'I'll have to go back home soon, Amy,' Wilbert replied, gazing at the rainbow.

'You do realize, my friend, that you can come back again and again.' Amy scuttled over to face Wilbert with Betty smiling where she was. Amy grinned and shouted into the sky, 'this isn't the end you know? This is just the beginning!'

Harpreet M Dayal was born and raised in London, England. She holds a BA in Business and Psychology from London Metropolitan University. The story of Wilbert's fear of the unknown very much mirrors her own fears of moving away from familiarity and comfort to somewhere new. Having spent all her life in England, she began the process of moving to Canada to start a new chapter of her life with her husband. This short book for children taps into the ideas of overcoming fears, standing up for your dreams, following your heart and accepting change.

Visit her online at: www.hmdayal.com

CPSIA information can be obtained
at www.ICGtesting.com
Printed in the USA
LVOW01s1951190816

500903LV00013B/44/P

9 780995 052703